Kindness Ninja

Written By
Brian Williams
Lynnette Bellin

DEDICATION

We would like to dedicate this book to our family, children, friends
and role models that have encouraged us to always seek out ways
to make our world a better place.

CONTENTS

1 Recruiting The Next Generation Pg 1

2 I Want To Be Like A Chopstick Pg 10

3 Planning The Missions Pg 18

4 Grumpy Pete Gets Grumpier Pg 24

5 The Opposite Of A Pickpocket Pg 31

6 Making the Grumpy Go Away Pg 39

7 Taking On The Winners' Club Pg 43

8 Bonus Message Pg 55

CHAPTER ONE
RECRUITING THE NEXT GENERATION

"Mooooommmm!" Brian yelled out the backseat window of his family's small four-door car, which sat crookedly parked on their short driveway.

"Hurryyyy! We're going to be late!" he pestered.

"I'm looking for my keys!" his mother shouted out the front door of the house.

Brian lived in a small red home at the end of a long cul-de-sac. He had one older brother and two dogs. His dad was a veterinarian, and his mom was one of the most amazing pastry chefs in the city. They were getting ready to go to karate class, which was Brian's favorite activity of the week.

Brian was a short 8-year-old boy, with unruly blonde hair and freckles scattered across his nose. He always wore a smile for everyone to see. He also had one of the world's biggest imaginations. To Brian, anything was possible. Sometimes he would even pretend that his hands were ninja swords, and would hand-chop everything in sight—

even tried to hand chop his birthday cake on his 4th birthday. (which made a big mess. . . but was pretty cool)

"Mom, I have your keys right here!" Brian yelled.
As she walked outside, she saw him dangling the keys out the rear window. She smiled and shook her head. Brian's older brother, Nick, followed her out to the car and got in the front seat.

"Mom, what do you think we'll do in karate today?" Brian asked as they rode down the highway.

His mother just shrugged her shoulders, focusing on the road.

"Think I'll get my next stripe?" he asked eagerly.

"We just got a stripe last week, Brian — we haven't even learned anything at the next level yet," Nick responded, looking back from the front seat.

"Well, once Master Tom sees that my hands are swords, he'll have to give me a stripe!" Brian said as he chopped invisible watermelons with his hands. The elderly lady driving next to them giggled as she looked over to see a child dressed in a karate suit hand-chopping the air.

Master Tom was their martial arts instructor. He had smile wrinkles so deep that he always looked like he was smiling at you, even when he was being serious. He always told his students, "I am not training you to become a black belt in martial arts. I'm training you to become a black belt in life." To Master Tom, karate wasn't just about kicks and punches— it was about being nice to everyone and *never* using your skills to do harm.

As Brian and Nick entered the karate studio, they both snapped their hands to their sides, stood at attention, and bowed to Master Tom before stepping onto the mat. Bowing was a sign of respect. It was like a karate version of a handshake.

"How are you two doing?" Master Tom asked the two brothers.

"Super good and getting better, sir!" they both exclaimed in unison. They said that to Master Tom at the beginning of every karate class.

Other kids in karate uniforms were arriving too, among them Brian's friends Brandon, Gary Joe, and Anna.

"Is everyone ready for class?" Master Tom asked loudly.

"YES, SIR!" all the students responded enthusiastically.

"Before we start, who can tell me the three rules of concentration?"

They all raised their hands.

"Gary, what are they?" Master Tom asked.

"Focus your eyes." Gary pointed to his eyes. "Focus your mind." Gary pointed to his head. "And focus your WHOLE body." Gary waved his hands in the air in a big circle.

During class, Master Tom had them kicking, punching, and dive-rolling across the mat. But at the end of class, he decided to have a friendly competition: a jump-front-kick contest! Who could kick the highest?

Master Tom walked over to the mp3 player, turned up the music, grabbed a sheet of thick paper and held it nose level in front of his face. The rules stated that every time you kicked the target (the piece of paper) Master Tom would raise it higher.

Brian hit the target three times but missed on his fourth try.

"Great job! Keep practicing," Master Tom said. "Now, go sit down and cheer on the rest of your team. Brian ran and sat against the wall, and began clapping his hands for his friends.

Gary Joe was up next. He could jump really high. He jumped so high, in fact, that Master Tom had to stretch his hands straight above his head while standing on his tiptoes. He couldn't hold the target any higher.

Everyone in the class wondered, *Okay, now what? There is no way Master Tom can raise his hands any higher than that!*

Then, like a light bulb switching on, Master Tom had an idea. He set the target down on the floor, walked over to Brian's mom, and asked, "Do you mind if I borrow your chair for a minute?"

She smiled and stood up.

"No way!" Brian yelled as Master Tom stood on the chair and raised the target over his head, almost touching the ceiling.

"Go, Gary! You can do it!" Nick yelled.

"We've got this!" the other students cheered from behind Gary. There were only two students who were still in the game.

Gary stared at the target and took several deep breaths. His eyes were focused like lasers on the target.

The entire room was quiet. Even the parents were on the edges of their seats. Everyone seemed to be thinking that there was no way a *kid* was going to kick as high as the ceiling.

Gary ran to the target, jumped up and flew across the floor— and just at the right time his kicking leg shot like lightning over his head. "Hiiiii-YAAA!"

BAM! He hit the target — and cheers exploded from everyone.

Now class was almost over. At the end of each karate class, Master Tom would circle everyone together for what he called the Word of the Week. He had a wealth of knowledge and stories that could fill a library. Each week, he would choose a story to share with the class.

This week, the story was called "Chopping Chopsticks."

"Do you think you could chop this chopstick in half?" Master Tom asked the class as he held up a single chopstick.

"Yes, sir!" everyone responded.

"Okay, how about this? Do you think you could break four chopsticks?" Master Tom asked.

"Um . . . Yes, sir," some students said nervously, wondering whether he would ask them to prove it.

"Okay, do you think you could break this many?" Master Tom asked as he held up a huge handful of what had to be at least thirty chopsticks.

Everyone in the class raised their eyebrows and shook their heads. "No, sir."

"We're kind of like chopsticks, said Master Tom. "Alone, we aren't nearly as strong as when we stick together. One of you tackling a problem or a project probably won't have the strength and power of a team doing the same work. One chopstick, SNAP! Thirty chopsticks sticking together? Unbreakable!"

Master Tom looked around at every student in the circle. "Okay, my young chopsticks, that was a great class! You all stuck together, cheering for each other, even when you were out of the game. That's teamwork!"

As Master Tom ended the class, he had everyone stand up and give a respectful bow. Then they all ran off the mat so the next class could start.

"Brian," Master Tom called out, "can I see you for a moment in my office?" Brian turned around mid-run as he was exiting the dojo, "Yyyeeeessss, sir?!?" he answered nervously, as this had never happened before.

Brian walked into Master Tom's office thinking of all the things he might be getting in trouble for. Maybe his mom told Master Tom about the laundry scattered across his bedroom floor? His bed not being made? Or for not sharing the last scoop of ice-cream last night with his brother? Brian was confused.

He sat in the chair in front of Master Tom's desk waiting patiently for him to walk in. While Brian waited, he looked around the room at all the pictures, awards and newspaper clippings on the wall. *Wow, Master Tom has done a lot of stuff,* Brian thought.

Master Tom walked into the room, took a seat and immediately opened his desk drawer. He took out a shiny black envelope, placed it on his desk so Brian could see it, and then looked straight into Brian's eyes.

"Brian, what I'm about to tell you must remain a secret. The only people you're allowed to talk to about this are your parents and myself. Is that clear?" Master Tom said in a serious voice.

"Yes sir," Brian answered.

"For centuries, there has been a secret society of martial artists around the world whose members have taken a vow to protect the integrity of the martial arts and the people in their community. They have taken their training out of the dojo and into the world. They don't rely on their kicks and punches -- they rely on their confidence, perseverance, integrity and humility. They are Ninjas. Kindness Ninjas," Master Tom explained.

Brian's eyes opened wide as he listened intently.

"Kindness Ninjas can hide not just in the shadows, but in broad daylight. They have taken a vow to help other people and to carry out kind deeds without anyone knowing it was them. They make people smile. They give people hope. They make people see the good in the world."

Master Tom held up a black envelope. "This envelope was left on my desk this morning. The black envelope only comes from the highest ranking Kindness Ninjas. . . It's funny, I've never even met them before," Master Tom said shaking his head in wonder.

"They snuck it into your office?" Brian asked.

Master Tom nodded.

"Brian, one thing you need to know is that there are Kindness Ninjas everywhere. Many of them will know who you are, but you won't know who they are. They are watching you. Testing you..." "Testing me for what?" Brian interrupted.

"Your name is in this envelope Brian." Master Tom said.

He opened the envelope and pulled out a piece of paper with metallic silver lettering.

> *Dear Brian,*
>
> *You have been chosen to become a part of an elite team of ninja warriors. We are ninjas that do good. We are ninjas that make people smile. We are ninjas that perform acts of kindness without being seen.*
>
> *Your mission is to recruit some of your most trusted friends to form a Kindness Ninja team. Over the next three weeks, we want you and your team to carry out ninja-style acts of kindness toward others. You need to remain anonymous. You need to remain hidden. We will be watching. We will be judging. We will be testing to see if you have what it takes to join us.*
>
> *Good luck & be kind.*

~ The Kindness Ninjas

Brian's face showed shock and excitement. Master Tom handed him the letter and he read it over to himself.

"Brian, this is a true honor," Master Tom said. "I've already spoken to your mother about this and she knows the responsibility with which you have been challenged. Good luck, and know you can always count on me if you need anything."

Brian stood up, gave Master Tom a respectful bow, and exited the office.

CHAPTER TWO
I WANT TO BE LIKE CHOPSTICKS

Brian left Master Tom's office in wonder and walked out of the dojo to meet his mother, who was waiting in the car.

"Master Tom told you about the letter?" his mother asked.

Brian nodded.

"I'm really proud of you, Brian. I think this is a great opportunity. Crazy to think that Ninja's are real. I never knew!" his mom said as she started driving home.

"Mom, that's because their Ninja's." Brian quickly responded

The next day, as he was riding the bus to school, Brian couldn't stop thinking about how he and his friends could become Kindness Ninjas together. Ideas raced through his head.

We could pay for someone's lunch, and leave a note saying it was from the Kindness Ninjas.
We could buy a book at the book fair for someone who doesn't have money.

We could leave money in a library book.

What a minute, Brian thought to himself. *Kind acts don't always require money. Besides, I spent all my money on video games last week!*

Before school started, Brian met up with his best friends, Sam and Anna. Anna had been in karate class with him the night before. As they huddled around, Brian said, "Guys! I have to tell you something, but you have to promise me you'll keep it a secret."

"What is it?" Sam asked.

"You have to promise!" Brian uttered.

"Pinky promise!" Anna responded, holding out her right pinky.

"Last night after karate class something crazy happened. I went into Master Tom's office and he gave me this letter." Brian slowly pulled the metallic letter out of his notebook with care.

As Sam and Anna read the letter their eyes opened wide. "What does this mean?" asked Sam.

"A secret society of ninjas has selected me to create a team of Kindness Ninjas to carry out nice things for people without getting caught. The members of this society are watching me, but I don't know who or where they are," Brian told them, still in awe of this challenge.

"Wait, like the society is full of real ninjas?" Anna asked as Sam was looking around to see if he could spot a kindness ninja.

"Yeah, Master Tom said so himself," said Brian. "I want you two to be on my team. But we have to keep it a secret. The only people who are allowed to know about this are Master Tom and my parents. But we only have a few weeks. Are you down to be on my team?" Brian asked hopefully.

"I don't know karate at all. I couldn't possibly be a ninja," Sam muttered, disappointed.

"You don't have to be. It's not about the kicks and punches. This is about being a ninja in real life. It's about having courage, integrity and humility . . . the true essence of the martial arts," Brian said wistfully.

"Well in that case, heck yes! Count me in. This sounds awesome!" Sam exclaimed.

"Me too," Anna chimed in excitedly.

The three of them smiled at each other, then headed off to their first class of the day. Ideas raced through their heads.

Sam was really tall for his age, and he was rail thin, as if his body couldn't keep up with how tall he had grown over the past summer. He loved baseball and had dark brown hair that he kept hidden under a baseball hat most days. Known for being a jokester, he always tried to make light of every situation. He didn't take karate but liked to pretend to karate-chop things when at recess with Brian and Anna.

During the morning recess, the three of them gathered to share their ideas.

"One time I helped a kindergartener find her classroom on the first day of school," Anna said, smiling at the memory.

"She looked so lost and was about to cry. It made me feel so good to help her find her way."

Anna was short —barely taller than a kindergartner herself —and had a smattering of freckles across her face and long brown hair that she usually tied back in a ponytail. On the days she wasn't in karate class, she was one of the star players on her soccer team, and loved a good challenge.

"That is awesome, Anna," Brian said "I've been thinking about how we could start the challenge. I was thinking we could team up to do a bunch of acts of kindness to complete within the next week or two. But remember that no one can know that we did it."

"Yes, like real ninjas, we have to keep our identities top secret," Sam interrupted. Then Brian did a karate chop and struck a ninja pose, loudly whispering, "SHA-SHHIIINNNG!"

"Sha-shhinnng!!" all three of them exclaimed as they did their best karate chops in the air. It was like their own version of a secret handshake or a pinky promise.

As Anna walked home from school that day, she couldn't stop thinking about what her first Kindness Ninja mission would be. She looked down at her feet while she walked, and then she noticed that one of the neighborhood children had drawn chalk flowers on the cement.

She stopped as she got an idea. Then she took off at a run to get home, and when she got there she called Brian.

"Hey, Anna," Brian said as he picked up the phone.

"How did you know it was me?" Anna asked.

"I'm a Kindness Ninja, remember?!" Brian responded, even though he had really just looked at the Caller ID.

"I have my first Kindness Ninja idea!" Anna exclaimed breathlessly. "We can bring sidewalk chalk to school and write secret kind messages all around the school."

"Dude, that's an awesome idea! How are we going to do this without anyone seeing us?" Brian asked.

"We have one person do it at recess, and the others will keep a lookout to make sure nobody is coming."

"Yes!" Brian exclaimed. "Tonight, I'll look on the Internet for some quotes we can use."

After Brian hung up the phone, he looked out his window and saw his next-door neighbor, Grumpy Pete, who was watering his rose bushes.

Brian never called his neighbor Grumpy Pete to his face. When they did talk, he would just call him Mister Pete. Pete's wife had died many years ago, and he lived all alone. Pete really hated it when kids were noisy, and considered anything above a whisper noisy. One time, Brian saw Grumpy Pete spray a kid with a hose because the kid had been yelling to a friend to wait up as they walked down the street.

Maybe Grumpy Pete wouldn't be so grumpy if people were nice to him, thought Brian. He usually just tried to stay out of Grumpy Pete's way, but Brian started to think that maybe he should try to win over Grumpy Pete with kindness. What a challenge that would be!

The next day at school, Anna showed up with a container of pastel sidewalk chalk, and Brian had a crumpled piece of paper on which he had written quotes he thought they could use. At their first recess, they met up with Sam at their usual meeting spot, which they called the Ant Hill, not because the hill had ants on it but because their school mascot was the anteater.

Brian and Anna briefed Sam on the plan.

"I love it!" Sam said after Brian and Anna explained what they wanted to do. "I'll be the lookout."

"What if we divide and conquer?" suggested Brian. "I'll head toward the basketball court, and Anna, you head toward the swings. Sam, if you see someone looking at us or walking in our direction, let out a loud whistle . . . wait, you *can* whistle, right?"

"Louder than a steam train," Sam said with a wink.

Brian carefully tore the crumpled piece of paper in two and gave Anna half of the quotes. He then did a karate chop in the air and said, "Sha-shinng!"

Sam and Anna quickly copied him, and they all struck quick ninja poses pretending their hands were swords.

Sam stayed on the Ant Hill, as it was the highest point on the playground. Brian had grabbed a few pieces of chalk from Anna and walked casually toward the basketball courts.

When he got there, he looked around to make sure no one was watching him, and then waved at Sam to signal he was ready to begin.

He looked at his half of the crumpled piece of paper, and the first quote was, "Be the change you want to see in this world."

He started writing in big letters:
B—E...
T—H—E
C—H . . .

All of a sudden, Brian heard a whistle, louder than a steam train, and looked up to see Sam waving at him, his face red from whistling so hard.

Brian leaped up and looked around—and saw that the kids who had been playing basketball had finished their game and were starting to walk toward him.

Not wanting to be caught in his first act as a Kindness Ninja, Brian walked toward them and nodded as they passed by.

"What is this?" he heard one of the girls say, beginning to read what he had written.

"Be the ch—?" she questioned her friends. "Do you know what that means?"

One of the boys she had been playing basketball with guessed, "Be the champions?"

Another girl in their group piped in, "Be the chin?"

"That doesn't make any sense," said the first girl.

They all shook their heads and resumed walking.

As soon as they rounded the corner and were out of sight, Brian ran back over and, scribbling faster this time, picked up where he'd left off:

A—N—G—E

He wrote this in big letters, and then, nervous that he would be caught, he wrote in smaller letters below it:

YOU WANT TO SEE IN THE WORLD.

He stepped back to admire his work and read it out loud: "Be the change you want to see in the world." *Oh, I need to sign it*, he thought. He then wrote, "The Kindness Ninjas."

Just as he finished, the school bell rang, and he ran toward his classroom. He ran into Anna in the hall.

"Did you do it?" he asked her.

She nodded.

"Which one did you write?"

"Smiles are contagious," she said, smiling ear to ear.

Brian smiled back. "Yes, they are."

They silently karate-chop-high-fived each other and then headed back to their classrooms.

CHAPTER THREE
PLANNING THE MISSIONS

At lunch time, the Kindness Ninjas gathered together.

"Two quotes on the sidewalk aren't going to get much attention," Sam commented.

"We should do it in our neighborhoods as well—that'd be easier," suggested Anna.

Sam's face lit up with an idea. "What if we left notes in books in the school library?"

"Yes, that's a great idea!" exclaimed Brian.

"I don't have soccer practice tonight, so I'll write some up after school on colored paper," offered Anna.

"And I can sneak them into the books on the library return cart in the hallway outside of the library!" Sam exclaimed.

That afternoon, while Brian was doing his homework at the kitchen table, he looked out the window to see Grumpy Pete shooing some birds off his front porch. Brian's mom was in the kitchen starting making dinner, and when she saw Brian looking out the window, she asked, "Something bothering you?"

Brian shrugged. "Why is Grumpy Pete so grumpy?"

His mom sighed and came over to sit at the table with Brian. "Many years ago, long before we moved into this neighborhood, Pete's wife and two children were killed in a car accident."

Brian's heart sank. He had always thought Grumpy Pete was just another grumpy old man, but now he realized how horrible that must have been for Mister Pete.

"He doesn't have any family in town," said Brian's mom, "and from what the other neighbors have told me, he lost all the joy in his life the day he lost his family."

"So that is why he doesn't like kids?" he asked.

She nodded. "I suppose seeing kids around the neighborhood reminds him of how much he lost."

"Mom, do you think I could do some Kindness Ninja treatment to Gr—" Brian stopped himself. "I mean, Mister Pete?"

His mom smiled. "I think that'd be great. Though, you know how Pete's favorite hobby is keeping track of everything going on in the neighborhood? Perhaps you shouldn't try to do this secretly."

Brian pondered this. He gazed back out the window at Grumpy Pete while his mother went back to making dinner. *Perhaps Grumpy Pete is the ultimate Kindness Ninja challenge*, he thought, not sure how he was going to approach this mission.

The next day at school, Brian got off the bus and started walking toward the entrance. He saw some kids gathered around, staring at the ground and talking. When he got closer, he saw chalk writing on the ground that read, "One small act of kindness can create a ripple." It was signed, "The Kindness Ninjas."

"Who do you think did that?" one fifth-grade girl asked another. The friend shrugged and responded, "I think it's kind of cool."

"Ha ha, an act of kindness is *kinda* cool," a fifth-grade boy scoffed.

It's working, Brian thought. *We got them talking. Now, what else can we do?* he asked himself silently.

The bell rang, and just then, Anna ran up to him and karate-chopped him playfully on the arm.

"You like?" she asked, smiling and gesturing at the chalk writing.

"I thought you might have had something to do with it."

"Yeah, my mom dropped me off early today because she had a meeting. There weren't very many kids at school, so I took advantage of the opportunity to get to work. I also wrote up some kindness quotes on colorful paper—take a look!" She unzipped her backpack and held open the pocket. Brian could see it was filled with small strips of colored paper.

"Anna, I'm so glad you're on my team — that is such a great idea! Give me a stack, and I can put some in books when my class goes to the library."

That day at lunch, the three Kindness Ninjas sat on Ant Hill plotting their next plan of attack.

"I was really thinking hard about what my kindness mission would be, "Sam said. I can't help but think of one of the girls in my class. Her name is Bonnie. Everyone knows she's really poor. I think that makes people feel uncomfortable to talk to her. Last week, we were asked to draw a picture of something we wanted to do this summer. Her picture was of her opening her own lemonade stand so she could earn money to buy her first bike."

"Wait, she doesn't even have a bike?" Anna said in astonishment.

"Wait, Sam. . . Didn't your little sister get a new bike for her birthday last year?" Brian asked.

"YES! No wonder we're friends -- you're thinking the exact same thing I'm thinking!" Sam exclaimed, smiling ear to ear.

"Wait a minute boys -- I'm confused!" Anna said.

"My sister still has her old one and it's still in perfect condition, Sam said. "What if we gave it to Anna as one of Kindness Ninja acts?"

Just then, a group of fifth-graders who liked to call themselves the Winners' Club walked up. They were known to be bullies and often liked to pick on Brian because he was smaller than them. They also liked to make fun of Brian for doing karate, because they thought the only cool sport was football.

The biggest of the boys was Brody, who was blond, strong, and liked to make girls cry because he thought it was funny.

Brody's two friends were Lewis and Jamal. They also thought it was really funny to make girls cry, usually by teasing them about their hair or their clothes. No one in the school messed with these three because they were strong and liked to get into fights.

"What's up, runt?" Brody teased Brian.

"Mastered any new ninja moves lately?" piped in Jamal.

Lewis did a few fake karate chops in the air to make fun of Brian.

Inside, Brian boiled with anger, but he also heard Master Tom's voice in his head, repeating the rule that he could only use his kicks and karate chops for good.

"Not much is going on," Brian said, forcing a smile.

"What are *you* smiling at?" Brody sneered.

Brian shrugged. "So how is football going this season?" he asked the boys, pretending to be interested.

"Well, we have to wait one more year before we're allowed to play tackle football. Flag football is okay, but I really can't wait to crush some guys!" Jamal said, squeezing his hands together like he was crushing an imaginary soda can.

"What's a little kid like you doing on the big-kid playground?" Lewis sneered at Anna.

Anna pursed her lips together. Nothing made her angrier than people making fun of how short she was.

Thankfully, the bell rang and all of the kids headed back to their classrooms.

"Why are you so nice to them?!" whispered Anna as they got out of earshot from the bullies.

Brian smiled. "That is what Kindness Ninjas do. Besides, if we're always nice to them, they'll get bored with us eventually."

He turned to face Anna. "I've decided that each of us should complete one more Ninja Challenge this week." I'm going take on one of the hardest challenges a Kindness Ninja could do. I'm going to win over my neighbor, Grumpy Pete. Sam is going to do something for the poor girl in his class. And you, Anna, are going to do something nice for the Winners' Club."

Anna opened her mouth in protest, but not a sound came out. She shook her head, turned, and bolted to her classroom, not wanting to be tardy. As she ran, she glanced back at Brian and shouted, "No way!"

CHAPTER FOUR
GRUMPY PETE GETS GRUMPIER

When Brian got home that day, he noticed that Grumpy Pete's newspaper was still in his driveway. *Not every act of kindness has to be secret,* Brian thought as he picked it up and walked to Grumpy Pete's door. Before he could knock on it, the door swung open.

"What are you doing on my property?" groused Grumpy Pete.

Brian was startled, but he held up the paper. "I just wanted to bring you your paper."

"Hmph," Grumpy Pete said as he grabbed the newspaper from Brian.

"Your roses are looking nice," said Brian. "The bushes are so big!"

"What do you want?" Pete muttered at Brian.

"Nothing. I was just thinking that since we're neighbors, it would be nice if I brought you your paper."

Pete grunted. "Well, you're making me miss my TV show." He closed the door in Brian's face.

I guess I'll have to do something BIGGER, Brian thought to himself.

As Brian walked into his house, the phone was ringing. He looked at the Caller ID to see that it was Anna calling.

"What's up, Anna?" he said as he picked up the phone.

"Seriously, how do always know it's me?" Anna laughed.

"I'm a ninja, that's what I do. What's up?" Brian shook his head, amused that Anna wasn't familiar with Caller ID.

"You're crazy, that's what's up! I don't accept your challenge," she grumbled.

"You don't have a choice," said Brian. "If you want to be a Kindness Ninja, you have to accept the challenges."

"You didn't tell me about any challenges when you roped me into this," muttered Anna.

"Life is full of challenges, Anna. It's what we do with those challenges that proves who we are."

"Well, I am *not* going to be someone who is nice to the losers in the 'Winners' Club.'" Brian could picture her standing with one hand on her hips and making air quotes with the other one.

"We don't know why those boys are so mean, Anna. We don't know what's going on in their homes. We don't know if they were picked on before, and that's why they think it's okay to pick on other people. But it's really hard to be mean to someone who is nice to you all the time."

Anna was silent for a moment.

"Are you still there?" Brian asked.

She sighed. "You sound like one of those salespeople on TV."

"But it makes sense, right Anna? I never said it was going to be easy to be a Kindness Ninja."

"I'll think about it," she muttered. "I've gotta go." She hung up the phone, and Brian smiled, encouraged that she would at least think about completing her challenge.

As he got off the phone, he saw Grumpy Pete pulling out of his driveway in his old Cadillac Deville. Suddenly an idea struck him.

I could trim his rose bushes! thought Brian. He knew exactly where his mother kept her clippers, and he was sure he could trim the rose bushes, clean up the mess, and get back to his own house before Grumpy Pete returned.

He ran and got the clippers. Then he ran back into the house and held back the curtains so that he could peer over at Pete's house. *All clear!* he thought to himself.

Brian ran to the front door, making sure that his footsteps were extra light—like a ninja's. He opened the front door and looked right and left to make sure that no one was coming. *This act of kindness must be done ninja style*, he thought to himself.

Then he darted out the door to the tree in his front lawn and leaned up against it, checking again to see if anyone was looking.

That's when he saw old Mrs. Norris walking down the street with her poodle. Brian stepped away from the tree, holding the clippers behind his back. "Hi, Mrs. Norris! Lovely day, isn't it?" Brian smiled as she walked by.

"Yes, dear. Lovely day it is," Mrs. Norris replied. Brian waited till she rounded the street corner, and then went back into ninja mode.

He ran over to Pete's yard and tried to determine where to start. The rose bushes were taller than him. He started with one bush, cutting back a branch and then cutting back others to match it. Then he started pretending that the clippers were nun chucks as he hacked at the bushes all around him.

When he got tired, he stood back and saw that two out of the four rose bushes were cut much farther back than the other two. "Hi-YAAAA!" he yelled as he once again pretended to defeat the rose bushes with scissor nun chucks. Once he thought the taller bushes were back to the size of the others, he stood back again. "Now they're smaller than the other ones!" he exclaimed.

So he cut back the original two bushes, and the next thing he knew, all of the bushes barely came up to his knees.

"Well, I don't think I can trim any more," Brian said to himself, admiring his work. He looked down at all the clippings on the ground, then noticed that Pete's garbage can was on the side of the house. He bent down to gather the clippings when he saw Pete's car turning down their street.

Brian quickly filled his arms with clippings and sprinted to the garbage can on the side of Pete's house. After he dumped the clippings in the garbage, he pressed his back up against the side of the house so as not to be seen. He heard Pete's car door open. Desperately wanting this to be a secret act of kindness, Brian eyed Pete's wooden fence and thought for sure he could jump over it to make a clean getaway.

Brian ran to the fence, jumped up and swung his leg over the top. He rolled over the top and landed with a thud. Then he turned jumped over the fence that connected to his yard and landed on the grass below. He got up, crouched in a stealthy ninja pose, and ran as fast as he could toward his own back porch.

Just then, he heard his mom yell out the back door, "Brian, dinner is ready!"

He dusted off his sleeves and pants and —limping slightly—walked into the house. He washed his hands and started setting the table as if nothing had happened. *Mission success!* Brian thought to himself with a secretive smile.

Minutes after the family sat down to eat dinner, there was a pounding on the front door.

Brian's mom answered the door.

Grumpy Pete stood there, red in the face and huffing.

"Who did it?!" he raged.

"What do you mean?" Brian's mom responded, confused.

Brian's dad walked to the doorway and stood behind her. "Is there a problem?" he asked.

"Heck, yes, there is a problem. Someone butchered my rose bushes, and I'm pretty sure it's that little . . . *rascal* . . . of yours." He pointed at Brian, whose smile had been wiped off his face when he realized that his act of kindness hadn't been received as he'd intended.

"I don't know what you're talking about," Brian's dad said firmly. "Brian has been home all afternoon, and I can't imagine him being remotely interested in butchering your rose bushes."

Pete glared at Brian, who sat silently at the table with his fork suspended in mid-air.

"You stay off my property, you hear?"

Brian nodded, at a loss for words.

Pete turned and stormed back to his house.

After the door shut, Brian's mom asked him gently, "Honey, did you do something to Pete's rose bushes?"

He nodded. "I was trying to do an act of kindness."

She smiled and sat down next to him.

"Well, in order to trim rose bushes right, you need to know what you're doing. I'm sure you meant to help, but I'm afraid you've made Grumpy Pete even grumpier. I'm not sure his rose bushes are going to recover from this."

Brian nodded. His Kindness Ninja Challenge had just become even more . . . . challenging.

CHAPTER FIVE
THE OPPOSITE OF A PICKPOCKET

The next day at school, Sam was walking through the halls with a smile strapped onto his face like a cape to a superhero. He pranced along looking left, looking right and turning all around to find Brian and Anna.

"Where are they?" Sam wondered. Then he heard Anna's laugh echo past him. Like a ninja, he turned around and instantly knew where it came from: the main entrance to the school.

As Sam rounded the corner to the main hall he could see Anna and Brian holding the door open for everyone as they walked into school. He walked over to them and leaned up against the door next to Anna. "Guys, I've done it," he said.

"Done what?" Brian looked across the doorway while giving some high fives to other kids as they walked in.

"My sister gave me her bike, and my dad dropped it off this morning next to the school bike rack. We put a bright pink lock on it and here's the code," Sam said, holding up a piece of paper with four numbers on it.

"Now all I have to do is sneak this code into Bonnie's backpack so she'll find it," Sam said.

"Perfect timing! There she is right there." Anna pointed at Bonnie, who was walking down the hall for class.

Sam took off like a bolt of lightning. As he got close to Bonnie, he slowed down to sneak up behind her. He reached out for the zipper of her backpack. Just as he was about to grab it, she turned and went into the girl's restroom.

Sam put his hand back down and stood there wondering how he could wait outside the girl's restroom without looking suspicious. He reached into his own backpack, pulled out a book, and stood there pretending to read it.

A few minutes later, Bonnie came back out and smiled at Sam. "What are you reading?" she asked. Flustered, Sam looked down at the book and realized he had been holding it upside down.

"Oh, nothing," he said, snapping the book shut and putting it in his backpack. Another girl came out of the restroom, and then she and Bonnie started down the hallway.

Sam took a deep breath and snuck up behind Bonnie again. This time he was able to slip the combination into the small pocket of Bonnie's backpack. Just then the two girls stopped walking to greet their old teacher, and then BOOM! Sam walked right into Bonnie.

"Uh, sorry," he said awkwardly and walked away quickly.

He rushed out to the front of the school, where Brian and Anna were waiting for him.

"I did it!" exclaimed Sam.

"Did what?" both of them asked.

"I put the combination in Bonnie's backpack. She's going to be so surprised!"

"Did you put a note on there with it that tells her what it is? Or did you just put random numbers on it and slip it in?" asked Brian

A nervous look quickly swiped across Sam's face.

"Oh my gosh," Anna exclaimed, "can you imagine how confused she would be to just get a note with four random numbers? Tell me, Sam, you put a note with it."

"Um . . . Um," Sam stuttered.

"You didn't, did you?" Brian said with a worried look.

"No, I didn't even think about that. I wanted to do something nice for her and didn't even think that far ahead. Gosh, the whole thing is ruined!"

"Don't worry, Sam. We can work together as a team," said Brian.

"Like chopsticks, we need to stick together on this one," Anna agreed.

"No, not like chopsticks, like ninjas!" Sam exclaimed.

"Like Kindness Ninjas!" Brian added. They all did their secret silent karate chop and began walking toward the playground.

"Okay," said Brian, "why don't we all sit down next to her during lunch? Sam and I can distract her by telling funny jokes, then, Anna, you can sneak a note into the front pocket of her backpack.".

"Brian, the only funny joke I know is, 'What do you call a bear with no teeth?'" said Sam.

Anna rolled her eyes. "A gummy bear. Sam, we learned that joke in kindergarten!"

"We're going to have to work on your jokes, Sam," laughed Brian "Don't worry, you can follow my lead at lunch."

As the lunch bell rang a few hours later, the three Kindness Ninjas grabbed their lunch bags and proceeded into the lunchroom. As they walked through the hall, they couldn't help hearing all the other students talking about the Kindness Ninjas.

"Did you see the sidewalk?" one student asked another.

"I heard the Kindness Ninja is ten feet tall and is a thousand years old," said a first-grader.

"Well, I heard the Kindness Ninjas can break an entire stack of bricks with their heads!" said another.

The three Kindness Ninjas looked at each other and chuckled.

As they walked across the lunchroom, they spotted Bonnie, their target, sitting by herself. She looked sad. "All right, team," said Brian. "Now it's our time to shine. Are you ready?"

"Ready!" said Anna and Sam.

The three of them walked through the lanes of tables, dodging the students standing up and sitting down. Anna sat next to Bonnie while Brian and Sam sat across from them.

"Hi. My name is Brian, and this is Anna, and, well, you already know Sam from your class. What's your name?" asked Brian, pretending he didn't already know.

"Bonnie," she said with a big grin.

"Bonnie? That's a beautiful name," Anna said. Bonnie's smile got bigger.

"Hey, Bonnie," Brian said, gulping down a bite of his sandwich. "Do you know what ninjas eat?"

Bonnie shook her head.

"ANYTHING THEY WANT!" Brian guffawed.

Bonnie smiled, not sure what to think of him.

"What do you get when you cross a ninja with a pig?" he asked, winking at Anna to let her know the coast was clear.

Bonnie laughed. "I have no idea."

"A pork chop!" Brian laughed, making karate chops in the air.

"Can you tell I'm in karate?" he asked her.

"I can!" she responded with a big smile.

Anna gave a sneaky thumbs-up to Brian to signal that their mission was complete. She had successfully slipped a Kindness Ninja note into Bonnie's backpack that said,

"Bonnie, you have been chosen for an act of kindness by the Kindness Ninjas. You have a surprise waiting for you on the bike rack. Use this combination to unveil your gift. You deserve it!"

As they got to know each other at the lunch table, they found out that Bonnie was one of four children, and that her mom was a single mother who worked at a local gas station. She also mentioned that she walks to school because her mom can't afford a bike for her. "It takes so long for me to get to school walking, but this summer I'm going to open up my own business— a lemonade stand. So next year, I'll have a new bike!"

Sam, Anna, and Brian shared knowing looks. They knew that they had performed the perfect act of kindness for Bonnie.

The bell rang, and the three Kindness Ninjas stood up and headed out to recess.

"Bonnie, want to come hang out with us during recess?" Sam asked.

Bonnie smiled again. "Sorry guys, I can't. I promised the librarian I would help her put away all of the book returns."

"Oh, that's so kind of you. Tell Mrs. Taliberry I say hello," Anna said.

As they got outside, Sam said, "Hold on a sec." He ran back inside and returned with a Frisbee.

"Hey, Anna, think you can throw a Frisbee as good as us boys?" Sam joked.

"I'm a ninja, of course I can!" she answered.

Anna, Sam, and Brian went up Ant Hill and stood in a triangle throwing the Frisbee to each other. After they stopped, Brian thought it would be a great time to ask his friends for ideas about what he could do for his next-door neighbor Grumpy Pete.

Brian told them the story about the newspaper and Grumpy Pete shutting the door in Brian's face. He also told them about the rose bushes.

"I don't know how to trim roses either," said Sam in an effort to make Brian feel better.

"Maybe you could knock on his door and just be honest," said Anna.

"What do you mean?" asked Brian.

"Tell him that you don't know how to trim rose bushes and ask him if he'll show you how. He may need a friend, and if that is what he enjoys doing, maybe he would like to teach you," said Anna.

"But what if he shuts the door in my face?" asked Brian.

"Dude, you're a ninja! You need to be brave!" said Sam.

That afternoon, while Brian was sitting in the kitchen having a snack, he told his mother about Anna's idea to get Grumpy Pete to smile.

"It's not a bad idea, Brian." She said as she was making herself a snack in the kitchen. "Besides, if he teaches you how to trim the rose bushes in his backyard, then you could also trim your grandma's. I'm sure she would love that!"

"What?! Are you serious?!" Brian exclaimed incredulously. "Grandma has a truckload of roses — it would take me a lifetime!"

His mom looked over at him and chuckled.

CHAPTER SIX
MAKING THE GRUMPY GO AWAY

As soon as Brian was done with his snack, he ran upstairs, threw his backpack on his bed, and looked out his window. He could see that Grumpy Pete's car was in the driveway. He paced nervously back and forth in his room.

Brian's mom came in and sat down on his bed. "Brian, what you and your Kindness Ninjas are doing is really special, and I'm proud of you," she said. Brian smiled.

"Kindness isn't always easy," she continued. "It takes bravery and courage. But you never know what small act of kindness someone may remember for the rest of their lives."

She rubbed his back and looked out the window, smiling to herself. "I remember when I changed schools in fifth grade. There was this boy—I still remember his name, Jeff Valentine—and he offered to show me around and sit with me at lunch. I didn't know anyone, but he introduced me to everyone he knew and really made starting at a new school much easier. That was a simple act of kindness, but I remember it to this day! Jeff and I remained friends all the way through high school."

Then she gave Brian a big hug and walked out.

Brian fantasized being a hundred years old and telling his grandchildren, "There is a legend of three ninjas, the Kindness Ninjas!"

He looked in his bedroom mirror, took a deep breath and said, "I'm a Kindness Ninja. I'm brave and I can do this."

He walked across his front yard and up Grumpy Pete's walkway and stopped to glance at the roses he had trimmed a couple days earlier. *Wow, I really do need to learn how to trim roses — they look horrible!* He thought to himself.

As soon as he reached the front porch, Grumpy Pete's door flung open.

"What do you want?" Grumpy Pete demanded.

Brian was so scared he couldn't speak.

"Can you hear me? I said what do you want?" Grumpy Pete repeated.

"I . . . I wanted to say I'm sorry for messing up your rose bushes. They always look so pretty, and I was just trying to help. I wanted to do something kind for you."

Brian took a big breath and continued. "I also wanted to ask if you could teach me how to trim roses the right way. I know my grandma would really like me to help trim her rose bushes too, but now I'm afraid I'll just mess them up like I did yours."

"Your grandma has rose bushes, huh?" asked Grumpy Pete. Brian could see the anger melting away from Pete's face, and even a hint of a smile.

"Yes," Brian replied, "a lot of them. She could open up her own flower store if she wanted. All different colors, too."

"Do you have gloves?" asked Grumpy Pete.

"I sure do!" Brian exclaimed. He reached into his back pocket and pulled out a pair of gloves he had borrowed from his dad.

"Those are a little big for you, but they'll do. Wait here and I'll be right back," said Grumpy Pete as he walked away to get himself a pair of gloves.

But right then, something magical happened. As Grumpy Pete walked away with his front door still open, Brian could see a reflection from the mirror above his woodstove of Grumpy Pete smiling ear to ear. He did it. Brian got Grumpy Pete to smile.

Once they got to Pete's backyard, Pete started telling Brian how to hold the pruning shears and how to tell the right place to trim the roses.

"My wife and I planted these together the very first year we lived in this house. These rose bushes are over fifty years old," Pete said wistfully.

Brian was in shock. He never knew rose bushes could get so old.

"How old are the ones in front?" Brian asked guiltily.

"Oh, those. I planted them last year. Don't worry, they'll come back to life after the horrendous haircut you gave them," Pete said with a chuckle.

Brian sighed with relief.

Pete smiled at him. "You remind me of my son."

Brian solemnly replied back. "I'm sorry about what happened to your family."

"It's nice to hear someone acknowledge my family," Pete said. "Most people prefer not to talk to me because they just don't know what to say."

Brian smiled. He made a mental note to have the courage in the future to say kind words to people going through a hard time.

CHAPTER SEVEN
TAKING ON THE WINNERS' CLUB

Monday morning came quickly and the three Kindness Ninjas were excited to see their sidewalk kindness quotes were still there. The three of them were swinging on the swing set before school started. Anna was swinging high. "Be careful, you don't want to go all the way around in a circle!" Sam teased.

"Bonnie! Hey, come over here," Anna beckoned as she saw Bonnie arriving at school for the day. Bonnie looked over and saw the three swinging and waving at her. She waved back and ran over to them.

"Did you see the sidewalk chalk in front of the school?" Sam asked Bonnie.

"Yes! I don't know who the Kindness Ninjas are, but they're awesome. Guys, I found a note in my backpack last night that said a surprise was waiting for me next to the bike rack!" she said, holding up the note excitedly. .

"What? Seriously? Did you see what the surprise was?" Brian asked.

"No, I only found the note last night as I was unpacking my bag," Bonnie replied.

"Let's go see!" Sam said and ran toward the bike rack. Brian, Anna and Bonnie quickly followed him.
"Wow, this is awesome, Anna said as the four of them ran across the playground.. Bonnie, how did they know who you are?"

"I have no clue. I just found it last night. I couldn't even sleep I was so excited!" Bonnie said.

When they all arrived at the bike rack there were four bikes locked up. "On the bottom of the note there were four numbers that must be a combination. *Guys*! Do you think they gave me a bike?" Bonnie asked.

"Why don't each of us take a bike and put in the combination to see if it unlocks any of the locks," Brian said.

"Great idea. Brian you take the green one. Anna you take that mountain bike. I'll take this one and Bonnie you take the red and pink one," Sam said making sure Bonnie was unlocking the bike his sister gave her.

Each of them crouched down with the locks in hand. "The first number is 6, Bonnie said. "Then 19 . . . 14 . . . and 2."

Each of them repeated the numbers in their heads as they put the combinations in.

"AHHHHHHHHH" Bonnie screamed. "It unlocked. It's a bike. A *real* bike." Bonnie yelled, jumping up and down with her hands in the air. The three Kindness Ninjas had huge smiles on their faces, knowing this was going to be a moment Bonnie would remember for the rest of her life.

BRRRRINGGG! The bell rang — it was time to go to class. "Quick Bonnie, lock it up, and make sure to not lose the combination," Sam said.

"Oh. I'll never forget the combination!!! Guys, they gave me a bike!" Bonnie said, still in shock.

As the four of them jogged back across the playground, Bonnie kept looking back at her new bike.

"These Kindness Ninjas are awesome!" Anna said to Bonnie while still jogging. "Whoever they are, they also attacked the library yesterday. There were Kindness Ninja bookmarks in all the books I returned. Mrs. Taliberry didn't see who did it, but she seemed to think it was a cool idea. Boy, are they super sneaky," she said.

Brian looked at Sam and gave him a ninja-style secret high-five for his good, sneaky work.

As they all walked briskly through the hall to their classrooms, Brian saw the Winners' Club out of the corner of his eye. He placed his hand on Anna's shoulder and said, "Hold up, Anna." They both stopped.

She scrunched her eyebrows in confusion, worried that they were about to be marked tardy for class.

"You said you were going to do an act of kindness for the Winners' Club," Brian said. "You said you—"

Anna interrupted him. "At first I didn't want to take you up on the challenge. But I'm excited to be a Kindness Ninja, and I can't be a big fat quitter. That would be like letting the Winners' Club win. Well, that's not going to happen!" she said.

"Soooooo, what are you going to do? If you want help, just ask," Brian said.

"I don't need your help. I figured it out last night," Anna replied.
"I remembered that my grandpa has a bunch of really old footballs from when he played in college. My grandpa was the star quarterback. He was practically famous. I asked if I could have one of them to give to a friend. Not only did he give me one— he signed it." She unzipped her backpack ever so slightly to give Brian a sneak peek at the brown leather football.

"Chip Johnson?!" Brian said incredulously as he read the signature. "Your grandpa is practically a legend in football history! That is so awesome!"

"Well, to me, he's just Grandpa," she said. "I've never followed football. But I guess it's cool."

"Cool?! No, it is freaking *awesome*! How are you going to give it to them?" Brian asked.

"Well, I can't do it ninja-style like the other acts of kindness. I want them to know it came from me. That way they might start being nice to us," she said.

"Anna! Hurry up! Class is starting," her teacher yelled down the hall.

They looked at each other, smiled and raced to class.

Anna's teacher, Mrs. Courtney, was short and had a bubbly personality. Her laugh was loud, and she always gave her students high fives as they entered the classroom each morning. Sitting on her desk was a giant box of prizes for students that she would catch being kind. Little did she know that she had a Kindness Ninja in her very own class!

Mrs. Courtney asked her students to each find a classroom partner for a writing assignment. "You have thirty seconds to find someone. Don't be last!" Mrs. Courtney said with a smile.

The entire class burst into motion. Anna quickly scanned the room to find Lewis, one of the boys from the Winners' Club. He was hurrying across the room toward his friend Brody. Anna needed to move even faster. So she ducked down, got on the floor, and crawled like a dog under all the desks. This way she knew she wouldn't have to dodge anyone, and she was sure to get to Lewis before he got to Brody.

"Lewis, I want to be your partner," she said, popping up from under the desks.

Lewis was startled. "But . . . but I was going to partner with Br—"

"Nope. You're my partner," Anna interrupted.

"Time!" Mrs. Courtney announced. Lewis looked confused, and Brody turned to the boy next to him to ask him to be his partner.

The class assignment was to come up with a story to tell the class. The story could be about anything. But not only did it have to have a beginning, a middle, and an end, they also needed to have a prop. Anna was excited, knowing that Lewis would love to make up a story about football, and she had the best prop hiding in her backpack.

"So, since you know a lot about football, I say we should make our story about football," Anna suggested.

"Really?" Lewis said, looking surprised.

"Why not? You do like football, right?" Anna asked.

"Well, yeah. But you're a girl, and girls don't like football," Lewis said.

"I may be a girl, but I love sports, and girls can like football too if they want. I just happen to prefer soccer, but heck—soccer is called football in some parts of the world! We'd better get started if we want a good story. So tell me, who is your favorite football player?"

Soon the entire classroom was filled with conversation from each team making up their stories. Anna and Lewis had fun writing about a girl on a high-school football team.

Once they were finished, Lewis asked, "So what should be our prop?"

"I happen to have the perfect prop in my bag," Anna said mysteriously. She walked over to her backpack and pulled out the football.

Anna handed the football to Lewis. It was faded brown from age but was still in very good shape.

"You have a football in your backpack?" Lewis exclaimed, amazed that a girl would be carrying around a football. He started tossing it gently from hand to hand.

"It was my grandpa's. He played football in college. This was one of the balls that scored the winning touchdown for a championship game," she said.

"You mean to tell me this is a college championship game ball?!" Lewis exclaimed as he put the football to his nose to smell the leather.

"Wait, it's signed!" he gasped as he noticed the signature scribbled next to the white laces.

"Yes, he signed it for me. His name is Chip Johnson."

Lewis's eyes lit up. "Chip Johnson?! I've heard of him! He was a legendary player!"

Anna nodded. "He has a *bunch* of old footballs in his closet. But he always says a football should be played with rather than collecting dust in a closet. I'd like you to have it. I actually asked him if I could have it because I wanted to give it to the Winners' Club. I'm sure you could use a good football to practice with on the playground," Anna said.

"You can't be serious!" Lewis said, incredulous. "But this is too special to play with!"

Anna smiled. "It's my grandpa's wish that it will be part of the game he loves so much, not sitting on some shelf collecting dust!"

"Wait, you . . . you really are serious?" His eyebrows furrowed. "Why would you do this for me after we made fun of you and your karate friend?"

"Because I know that, deep down, you're a kind person," Anna said. He smiled shyly. "I also know that one kind act usually inspires another, so think of this as a kindness challenge . . . tag, you're it!"

"Okay, awesome! No, you're awesome!" Lewis exclaimed. "I'll totally pass it on—that is such a cool idea." He stood up and waved at Brody to get his attention, loudly whispering across two rows of desks, "Brody, look what Anna just gave us—a real signed championship game ball from Chip Johnson!"

Brody mouthed, "No way! Chip Johnson? That's awesome!"

Right then the bell rang for recess. "Okay, class, we'll continue the lesson when you get back," said Mrs. Courtney.

The three Kindness Ninjas met on Ant Hill and looked down on all of the other kids playing on the field. "I see the Winners' Club has a new football," said Brian.

Anna smiled. "You know what? They aren't that big and mean after all. They just needed a little act of kindness," she said.

Just then, a group of girls walked past the Winners' Club. On any other day, the boys of the Winners' Club would have teased the girls, but today, Lewis just yelled out, "Hey, Jenny! Your shoe is untied!"

Jenny stopped and looked at her shoe, wondering if Lewis was playing a practical joke on her. But she saw that her shoe really was untied, and kneeled down to tie it. "Uh, thanks," she said, obviously surprised.

"Did that just happen? Normally they would have just waited to see her trip and fall," Sam said.

"And then laugh at her," Brian chimed in.

"Team, we did it. We all accomplished our Kindness Ninja missions and made a difference. Bring it in."

The three Kindness Ninjas made a circle, put their hands in the middle, and yelled, "Shaaa-shing!" Then they jumped up into the air with a loud "Hi-YA!"

Their first Kindness Ninja Mission was now complete. As Brian walked home from school that afternoon, he couldn't stop thinking about what else the Kindness Ninjas could do, and he couldn't wait to report back to Master Tom about his success in creating mysterious superheroes of kindness.

As he turned up his street, Brian noticed some chalk drawings and writing on the sidewalk. He paused and saw that someone, obviously a really young kid, had written: "Be Nis." There was also a smiley face that said next to it, "Smiles are free." Brian smiled, sure that some kindergartner or first-grader had been inspired by the Kindness Ninjas.

As Brian walked up to the front door of his house he saw a black envelope taped to the door. It was the same type of envelope Master Tom had on his desk. Brian dropped his backpack and opened the envelope as quickly as he could.

As he pulled out the note, it was written in the same metallic ink as the one Master Tom had.

Dear Brian,

We have been watching you. You have impressed us with your creativity. Sam and Anna make a great team -- you chose them well. This is only the beginning -- we want to see more.

Good Luck & Be Kind

The Kindness Ninja

Brian smiled broadly. Rather than go inside, he turned around, walked over to Mr. Pete's house, went up to the front door and knocked. When Pete opened the door, he grinned.

"Hi, Pete!" Brian exclaimed. "If you're not busy, I'd love to hear more about your family. I'd especially like to hear about how I remind you of your son." Tears welled in Pete's eyes. "I would love to talk to you about that."

"Great!" said Brian. "But first, let me run home and tell my mom where I am. I'll be right back!"

Brian sprinted next door and told his mom that he'd be visiting Pete for a while.

"Pete?!" his mother exclaimed, surprised.

"Yeah!" Brian said. "And can we go to Grandma's this weekend so that I can trim her rose bushes?"

He could hear Master Tom's words in his head as he rushed back to Pete's house. *This week, I want you to be like chopsticks. I want all of you to do acts of kindness with some friends. It is a simple act of kindness, done in solidarity, which can create the massive change we seek.*

He chuckled as he thought, *And we didn't even need ninja masks.*

Brian's mom smiled as she watched him run to Pete's house. She glanced down and saw a spiral notebook that was left open on the kitchen table. Curious, she moved closer and saw that it was a check list, with each item checked off as complete.

Kindness Ninja Challenges
1. Kindness quotes written in chalk at school and in neighborhoods
2. Secretly give Bonnie her first bike. (Boy, was she excited!)
3. Kind quotes in library books.
4. Win over the Winners' Club.
5. Make Grumpy Pete less grumpy.

The possibilities for the Kindness Ninjas were endless, and, like any good superheroes, Brian and his friends looked forward to their next challenge.

ABOUT THE AUTHOR
BRIAN WILLIAMS

Brian started martial arts at the early age of 4 years old in Reno, Nevada under Master Ernie Reyes Sr. and Tom Callos. Now, 30 years later, he travels the country motivating audiences of all ages to carry-out daily acts of Kindness. He is the founder of Think Kindness, a non-profit organization that inspires measurable acts of Kindness in schools and communities around the country. He has spoken to over 350,000 students, collected over 300,000 pairs of shoes for needy children around the world and has raised over $250,000 for local and global causes. Now his life mission is to inspire Kindness Ninja's around the globe!

ABOUT THE AUTHOR
LYNNETTE BELLIN

Lynnette is a karate mom of her very own little ninja. She is on the board of Think Kindness, and has made it her life's mission to raise her two children to be kind, and to help inspire kindness in others. This is Lynnette's fourth children's book, the first three were a series called the Adeline's Magical Moments Collection Lynnette also owns and manages Reno Moms Blog, and works in content marketing.

BONUS MESSAGE

Dear Reader,

We need more people in the world just like you! We need your courage, strength, but most importantly, your kindness.

I have a special gift just for you. If you would like to carry-out your own Kindness Ninja challenges then you'll love what we have in store for you.

GO VISIT: www.KindnessNinja.org/mygift

You may need your parents to help you complete the needed information to make sure I get everything too you. But this will be your first step in becoming a *Kindness Ninja!*

Good Luck & Be Kind.

~The Kindness Ninja's

Made in the USA
Middletown, DE
25 August 2019